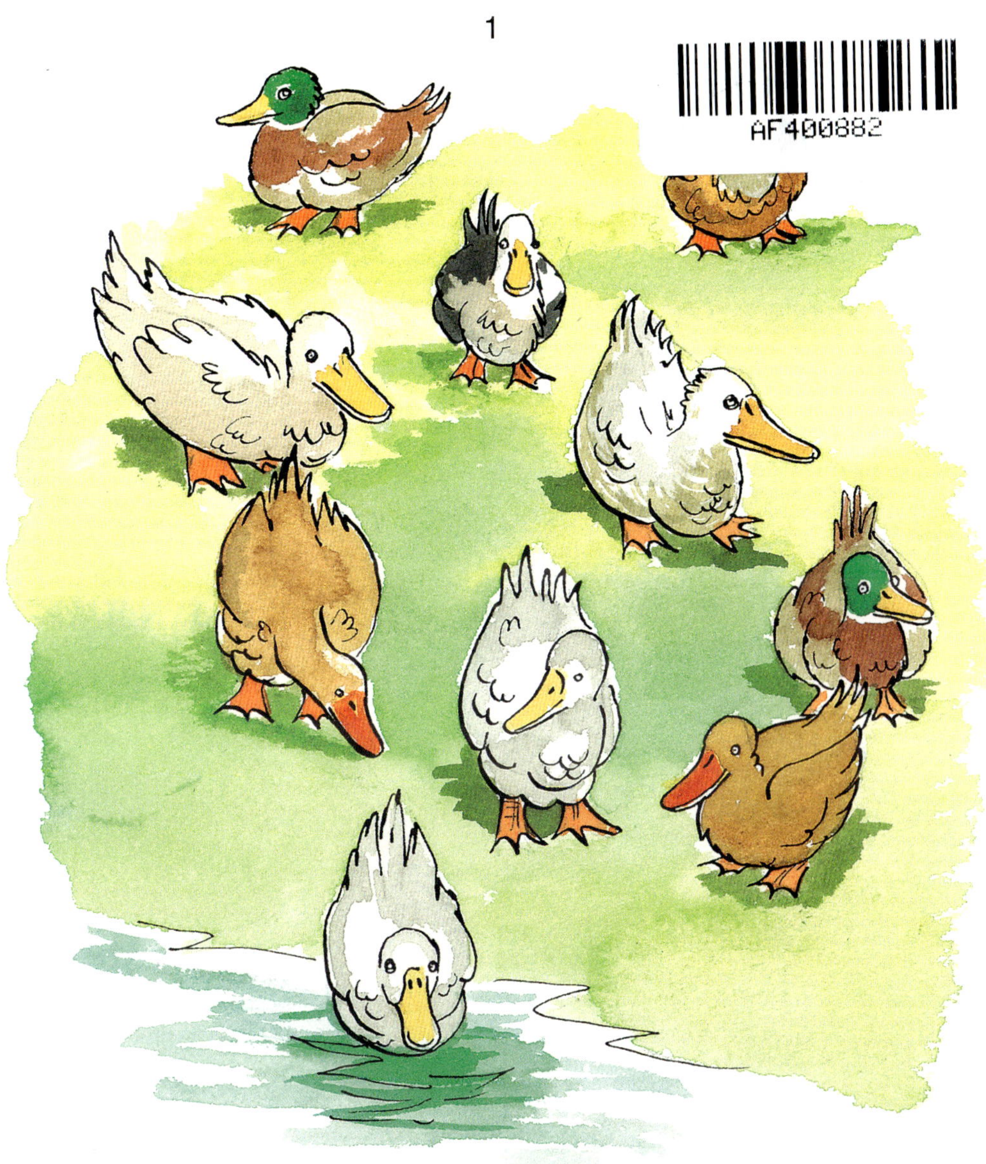

Ten ducks.

Ten ducks swim
on a big pond.

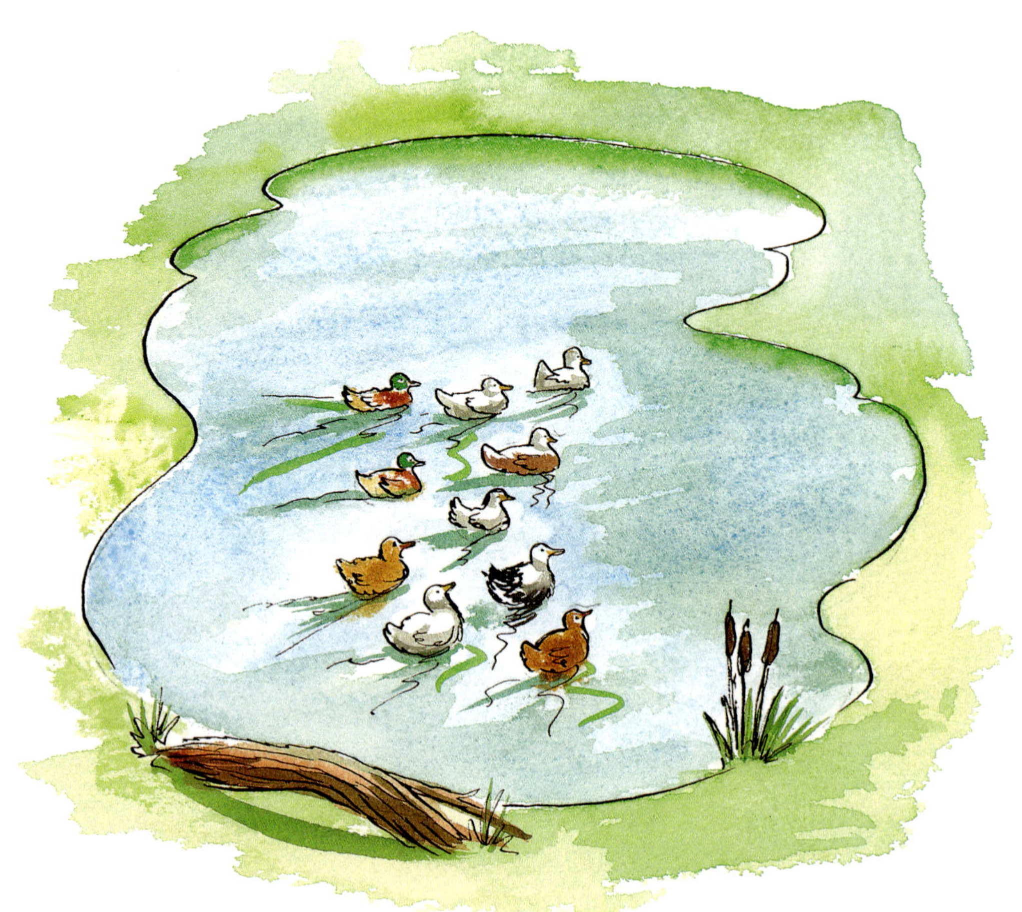

A big green frog.

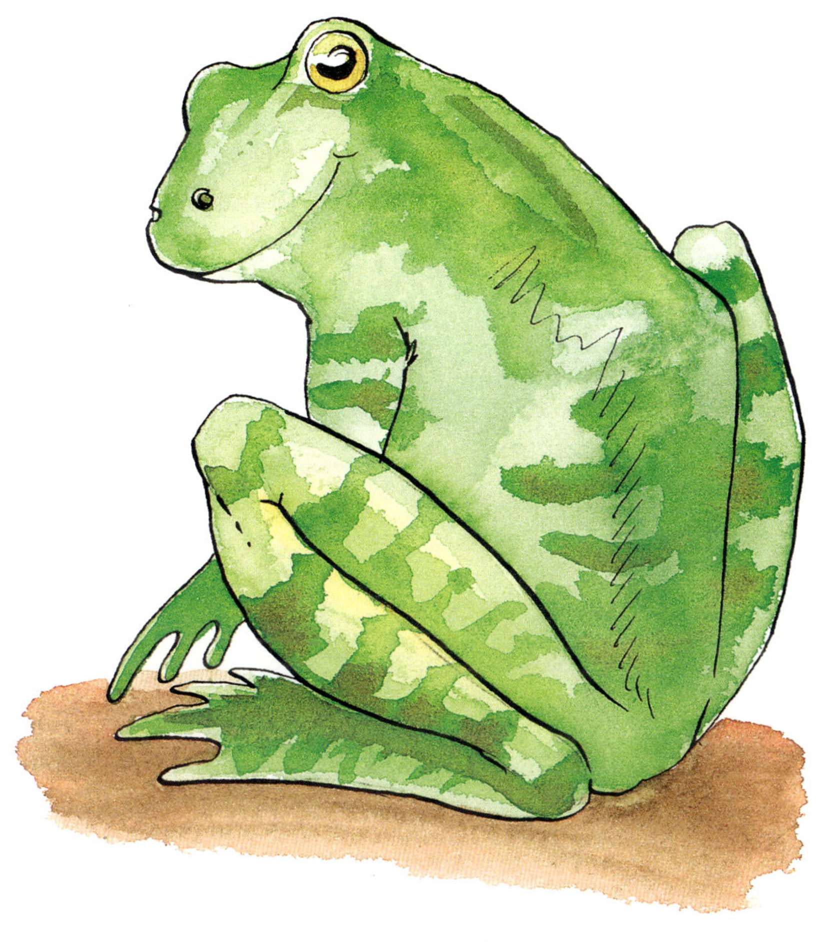

The big green frog

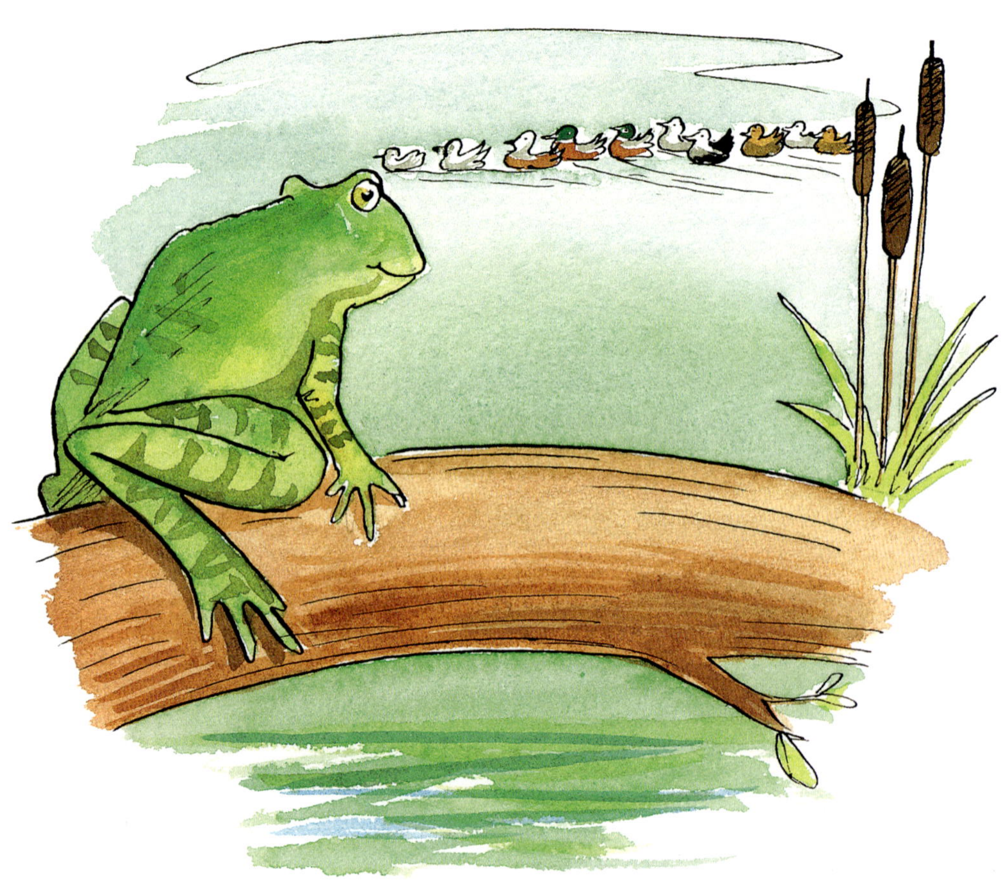

sits on a log.

Then the frog

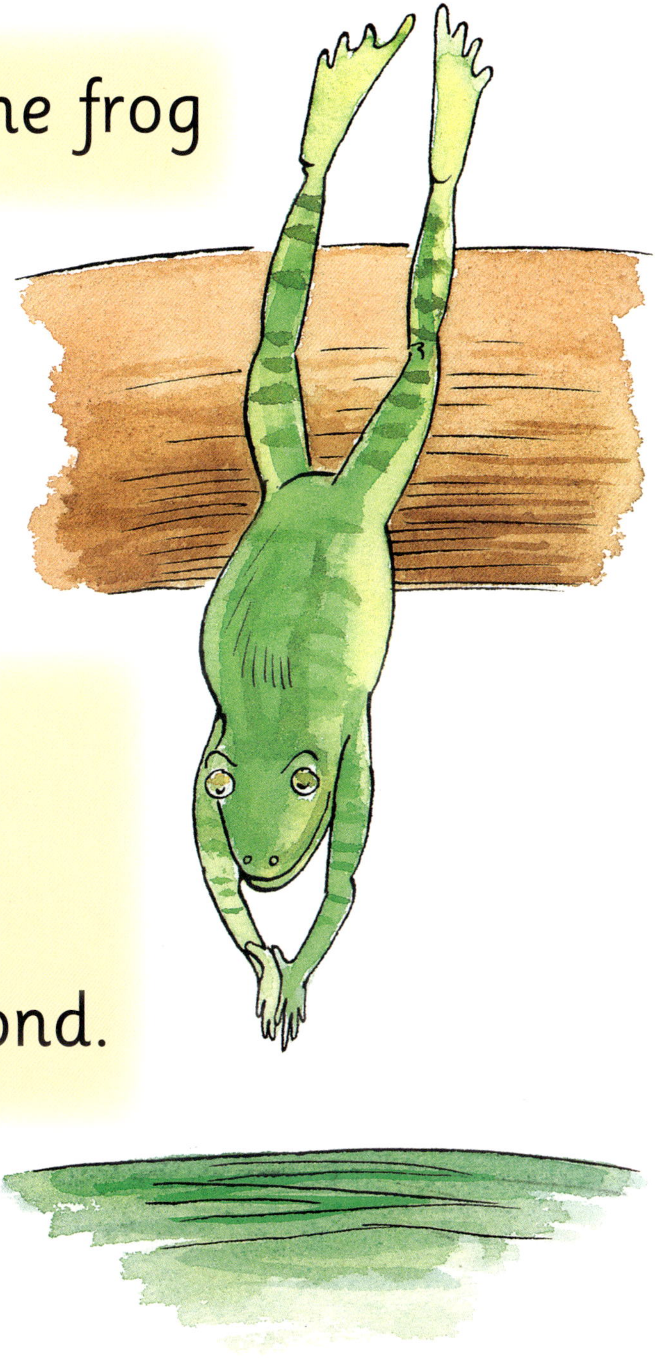

jumps
into
the
pond.

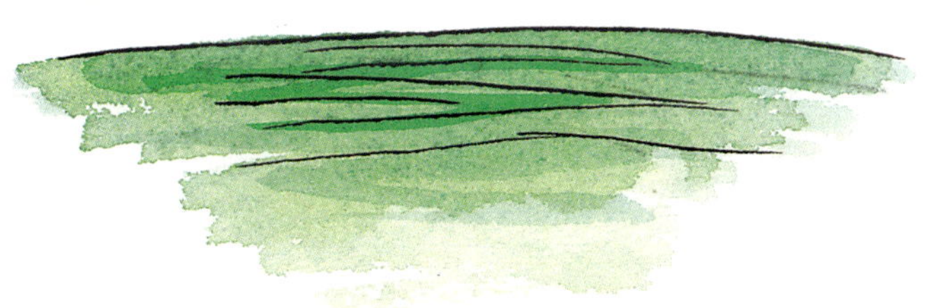

He lands with a loud

splosh!

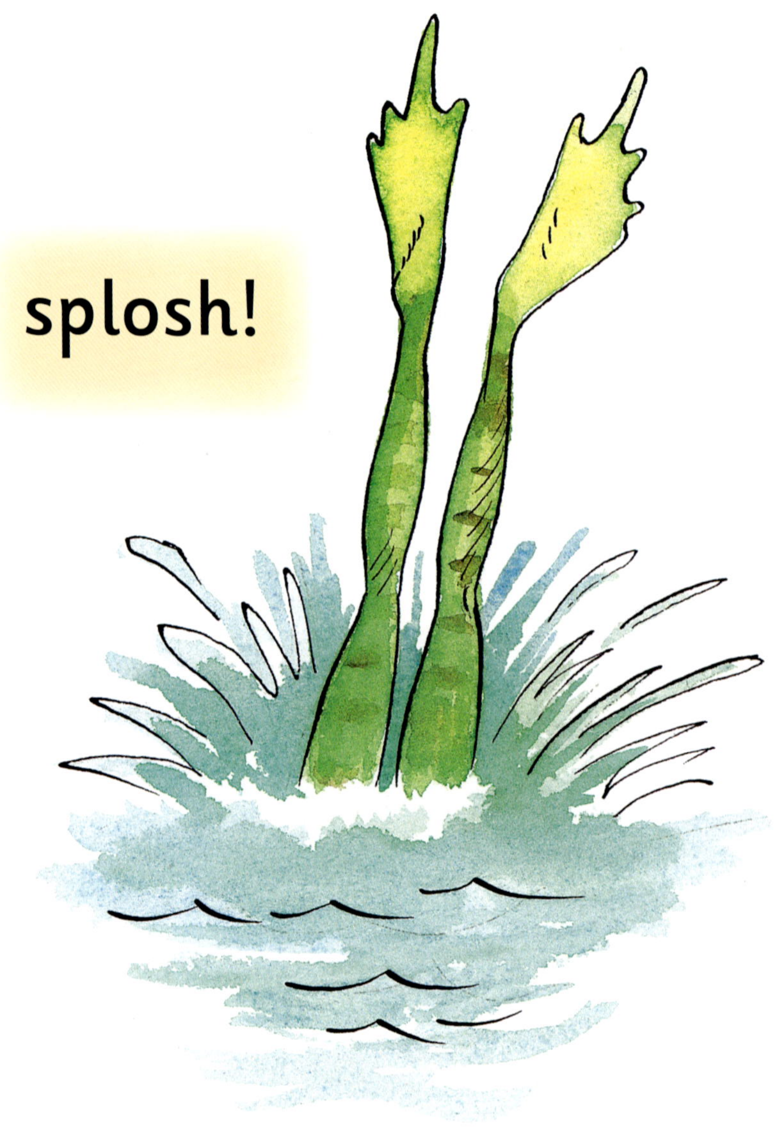

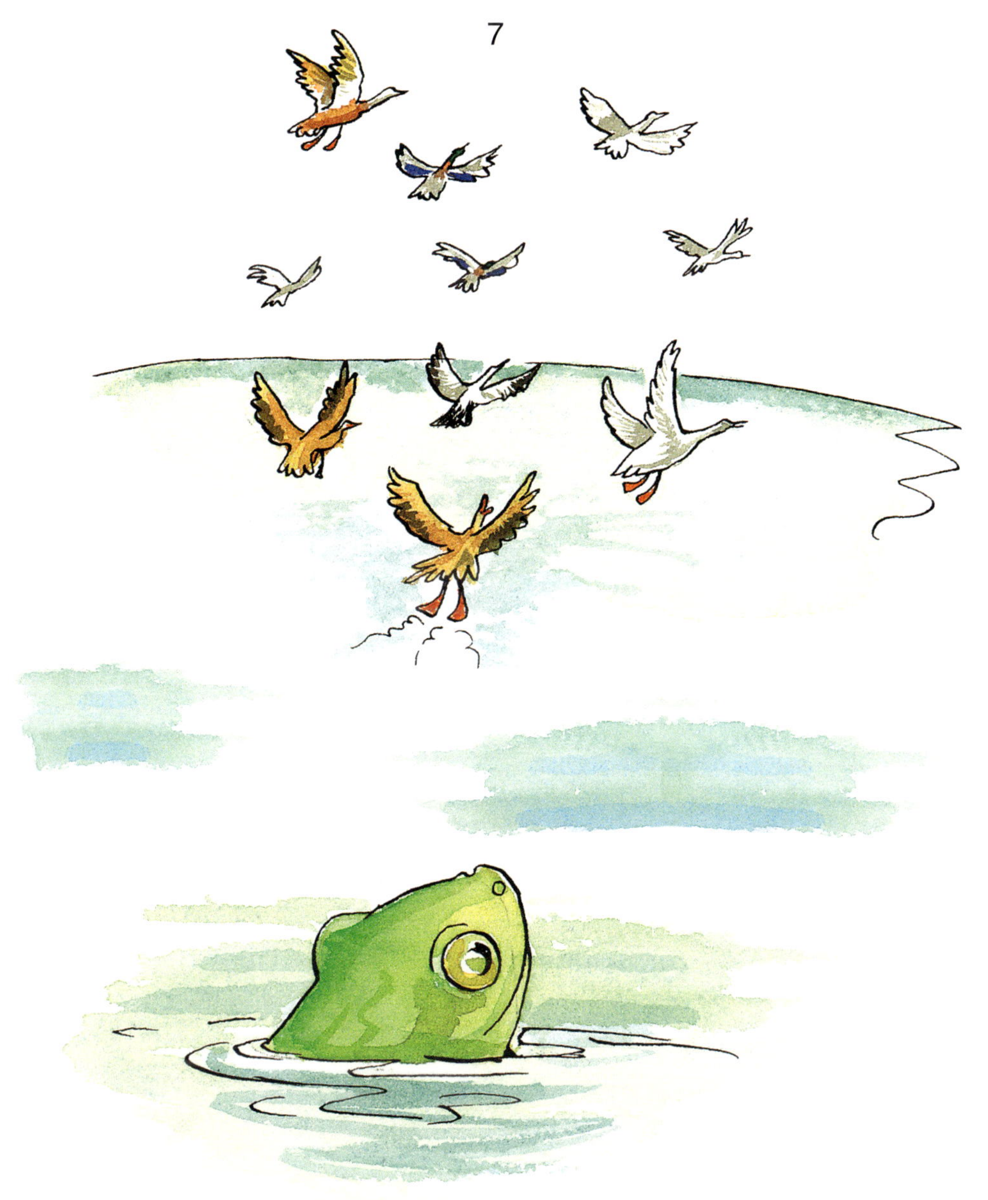

The ten ducks flap off...

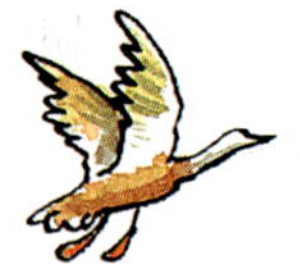 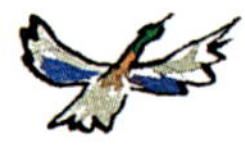 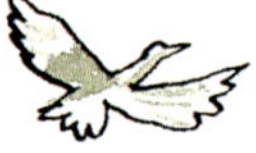 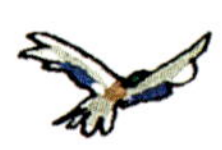

...and the frog has the big pond to himself.

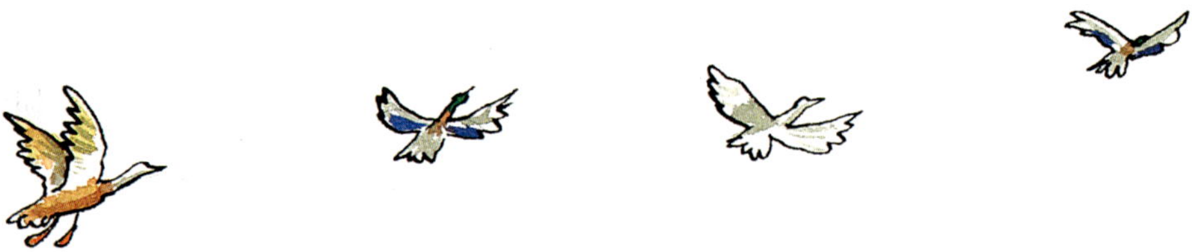

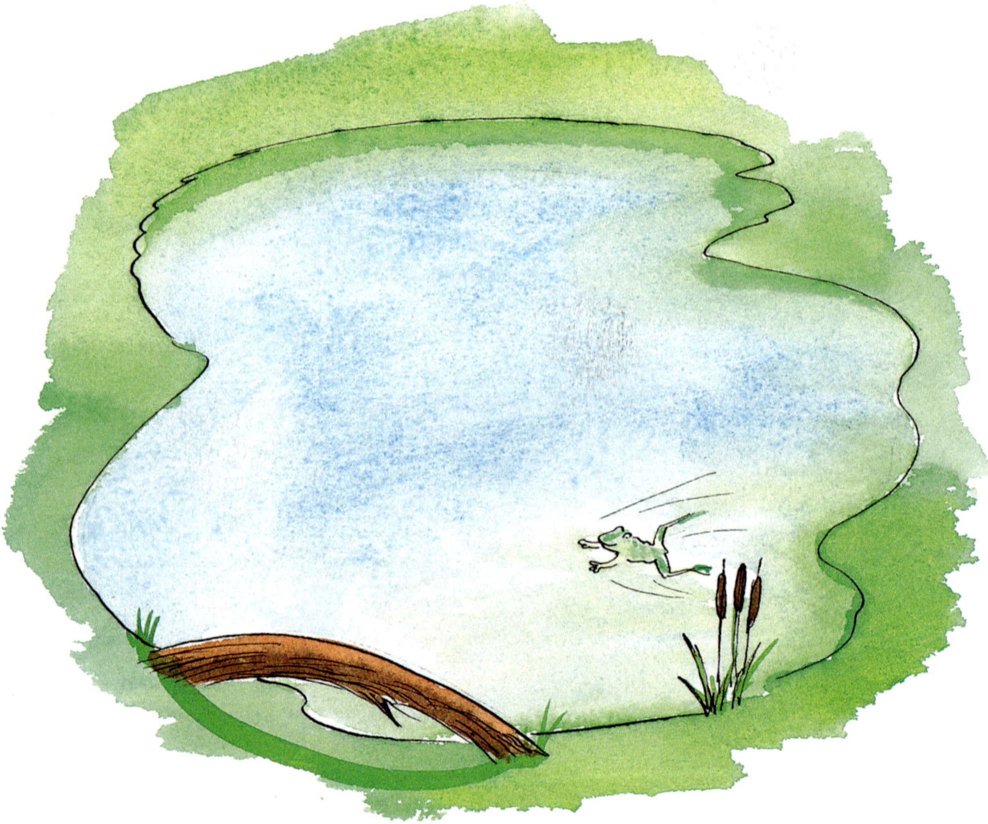